AF448381

Notes / Ex

A note from Lagard the Unseen; 2028AD on events in 2000AD

To those skilled enough to find their way into this document.

I am not an artist. Quality thieves, and those posing as them, always claim they are. They like to think of themselves as above riff raff pick pockets and thugs. They shroud themselves in the illusion of sophistication while simultaneously taking from those who have earned what they own. Make no mistake, you and I, we are just plain thieves. We riffle through other people's things and take what we can get away with. Until you accept the bottom feeding nature of this profession you will never become great.

Don't get me wrong. I love what I do, and I do concede there is an art to the skills I employ, but there is a science too. I have always viewed myself as wielding art and science to carry out tasks that are generally unethical for my own gain. I think it is this double use of science and art, coupled with the appreciation for exactly how inglorious my life choices are, that have allowed me to gain so much. I believe it was Plato that spoke of leaders in ancient Rome… Greece… lets go with Europe… needing to be at the apex of art and science. Well, in a Platonic sense, that makes me a leader, or to be technically correct, THE leader of Earth's leading thieves guild.

I would like to tell you a tale. One that I have experienced recently that has opened my eyes as to the significance of our skills and one that gave our guild the edge it needed above all other robber guilds. There are many who wonder why a society which has no concept of currency and little regard towards material gain would have such a thriving criminal underground. Well I will tell you now it is because no matter how you resort a culture, no matter how perfect you build a society, there will be some who have something that someone else wants. Whether it be power, a mate, or some un-replicatable item, someone will always have a thing someone else wants. The question is how far will your society go to suppress that?

Don't get me wrong, the SA is filled with good, upstanding people. They are motivated with pure intentions derived by a common history, culture, and the choice to make mistakes. And that is where lies the problem isn't it? It is our ability to choose to do stupid things, to give into our desires good or ill that ensures the criminal element of the SA will ALWAYS exist. There is a quality to us, the lack of necessity, the subtle brutality of the SA, that makes our community the best and most fearful underground in the Galaxy. My story will drive this concept home, but make no mistake, we, the underground, have our beneficial uses in society.

It was on the eve of the millennium turning that this story began. I was on Nexus at a "seedy" tavern, well at least seedy as far as the Cluster Civs knew. They call them bars in the Cluster, and even the worst among them were about on par with the average underground Infernal club. I was sitting at a metallic counter that wrapped around a central alcohol station shaped like a jagged star. It meant that when people sat at the bar, instead of staring at the center, they were just as much looking at the patrons across from them. This bar was designed as a somewhat innocent social club that brought together strangers and lonely travelers. As the years passed on and the owners exchanged hands, the place descended into a neutral headquarters of criminal organizations. Big and small they could gather here and discuss business, make deals, and sign contracts to kill each other.

The atmosphere of the place still retained it's original innocent fun though. The bar's surface shimmered with iridescent lights that reacted to touch or when a glass was placed on it. The alcohol behind the counter was hanging like a chandelier and was colorfully lit as well. The outside border of the cavernous room had several levels, room for dancing, and many private booths.

I was drinking at the bar, not being noticed. I had taken an alcohol inhibitor, so getting drunk was not an issue. I heard someone walking up to me. He smelled like smoke. When he got within five feet he paused and spoke with a deep voice. "Human" I have both Elven and Human blood in me, but it mattered little, I knew he was speaking to me. I also knew he was not someone looking for a random fight, but someone looking for me. I have a tattoo that helps me blend in and stay very mundane. If someone comes up to me, they have to be looking specifically for me.

I turned on my chair to face him, looked into the Braxin's eyes and asked with a somewhat hostile tone "What?!"

He stepped back a bit as if afraid he had offended me by not using my name and said "I just didn't think you wanted your name used... He will see you now... sir.

I stood up facing him, patted him on the shoulder "Don't worry about it, just let's go." I had to keep my emotions in check here. I didn't realize that I was in such a bad mood sitting in this bar, but if I started flying off the handle this meeting would not end well. People who were powerless were allowed to rage and intimidate these criminals, fighting for position in a made-up social hierarchy. I on the other hand was already perceived as a predator just by being a Terran. To be in charge of a major Terran guild put me on such a high standing, if I lost my temper or patience with these savages they would run for the hills or fight me like a cornered and scared animal. I am not exaggerating with that. I was there for The Red Hand's terrible negotiation disaster several years ago, and I assure you Grog wasn't even angry, he was just joking. Grog's fighter for hire guild is just now able to make cluster meetings in person again.

My escort eased and lead me out of the center area of the bar. We moved towards a private booth on the outer edge. The booths were made to be... very... private. They were originally designed for travelers to get to know each other a bit better, but that quickly degraded into a thriving sex trade. Gangs took control after that, creating some organization, turning them into drug and prostitution dens. As I suggested earlier, the syndicates wedged the gangs out, restoring this place to its original cleanliness. The booths were now places private deals could be made.

We passed through a curtain which opened up to an area too large to be considered a booth. It was more a private room with seating and small side tables. Inside were various species with equally varied dispositions. Some were there to intimidate, and others were there to look good. Sitting in one of the corners, next to an empty seat was a Fex who went by the name of Irate. I kid you not. Fex criminal lords tended to take names like Dragons do, after emotions that embody them. Unlike the Drago though, the names infrequently gave an accurate portrayal of their true personalities. They were mostly there to intimidate, and this guy was "known" for loosing his temper at people who disagreed with him. Around each other at least we kept our fearsome reputations at the door and neither one of us had ever lost our tempers in front of the other.

I was guided to the chair next to Irate by his Fex "Personal" assistant. She was barely wearing anything but that never made any sense to me on a Fex. She had so much fur across her body, I wasn't sure what was being covered up. Irate seemed to appreciate it though and he stared at her as I took a seat. That behavior was sloppy of him and something I had taken note of since I first met him. He had a weakness for trashy women.

I sank into a chair that was considered comfortable by Cluster standards. As I settled in, a Kek came up to me holding several trays with his tentacles, each tray having either drinks or food. The Kek looked like some downtrodden Jans slave but I knew better. Not many could tell the difference between Kek, but I could tell by the colors and shapes of his patterns this was Sipsin the Hatchet. Likely one of the more feared Cluster hitmen. Let's just say he was not known for clean slayings and was paid very well to send messages. Did Irate even know who his new servant was? I had a feeling one of Irate's rivals had sent Sipsin undercover. I thought about warning Irate. I thought about killing the Kek right there. I decided a long time ago to not get involved with such things in the Cluster. Let you not be mistaken, we have no friends in the Cluster. They all distrust us, they will all exploit us, and most importantly, they will all betray us. Granted I always get more cynical the longer I work in the Cluster.

I did not take any drink or food. Irate smiled, but he was always a little uncomfortable around my style.

He broke the silence "I have the jobs you requested".

I turned to him and responded with no humor in my voice "Alone"

He knew for some time I insisted on having my meetings with him alone, but time and time again, he acted as though he forget this. It was as if Irate was so in the habit of showing off his retinue we were going to repeat this silly game forever. The crime boss nodded to his people and they all filed out.

When everyone left, he said "Always down to business with you. Would it kill you from time to time to relax?"

I responded with a serious tone "Yes" I cracked a smile and we both laughed a bit at this. I then said "Criminals don't get resurrections"

He squinted in confusion at my statement, and figured it was an SA joke he didn't get, so he just laughed some more.

Irate handed me a computer chip. "There are fifty-six jobs here. All legitimate. None of them SA traps." Fake missions had been on the rise by some malicious parties bent on capturing SA natives. No idea why, even if they managed the feat, the Huntsman guild was called in, much to the guild member's delight... Irate had been acquiring missions as a third party for me so no one knew they were for SA citizens.

"Good" I took the data chip. "I hope a few of these are challenging. If they are anything like the last set, my people will start softening up. I will have to rotate them back to the SA."

The Fex smiled "Typical SA arrogance." He laughed putting his hands up as if to say that he would not impugn my honor any further, even out of fun. "I would not scoff at these. I assure you they will be challenging, even by your people's standards."

I nodded "Thank you."

"Of course, what are friends for!" He smirked as if knowing this would never be true. That being said, he knew he had become valuable to a rising underground element of the SA. "I must ask, why do you send your minions on these dangerous missions? There must be better ways to scam the Cluster out of currency."

I smiled as if getting a joke he had not. "Even after all this time Irate... I am disappointed. First, they are not minions, it is not wise to use that phrase around our kind. Unlike Cluster crime organizations, people don't join SA underground guilds out of necessity. Our members are all independent agents and can leave at any time." I was mostly telling the truth here. To be honest, most underground guilds are not as lucky as we are to provide such freedoms. Many join underground guilds out of desperation and greed, and find it difficult to get out. Our guild on the other hand has flexible enrolment and I strongly suspect that some members of the SA leadership use us to get experience for their agents. I am not saying they would be complacent in crime, but I also know we are not as pursued as some. "Second," I continued "I like organizing this for my people. It gets them experience with non-SA targets."

He thought about this answer for a moment and responded "Well, perhaps my business model is not as free as the Illusive Hand's, but we still enjoy what we do. I make sure my people are well taken care of. When my people are not safe, I am not happy... which brings me to a mission I have that is not in that chip."

Not in the chip meant not willing to get it traced back to him. It was easy to be a middleman and hand over a chip with a collection of jobs, it was quite another to ask for a personal task. I had a feeling what was coming next worried Irate deeply.

"I..." He awkwardly began "have an issue. One I want you to take care of. A rival is causing some issues, some of my people are winding up dead, and I need this individual to no longer be a threat."

"Hey" I objected "I don't do those jobs. You want to intimidate and dice someone to bits, you ask the Bloody Hands, you want it clean you call on the Subtle Wrists, but my group we just steal."

"Why do you SA criminals always have the name hand or finger or some such other body part in your name?"

"It's a long story, but think of us as an extension of our clients, our clients that don't want to get their hands dirty, but again, I don't get my hands dirty that way."

He shrugged and continued with his hands up as if he were trying to slow down the conversation "Fine but calm down, I am not asking for you to kill someone. I am asking for you to steal something so critical to my rival it will eliminate him as a threat."

"Well that is something else." I relaxed back down into my seat not realizing I had begun leaning forward in my chair. "Sure Irate, I have some very good people I can get to carry it out, for the right price."

Irate pointed at me as he said "No Lagard… this one I want you to handle personally."

I must have had a shocked look on my face because the crime lord fell silent, as if waiting for my next response. Leaders of underground guilds took jobs, don't get me wrong. We are not like crime syndicates of the Cluster, who's leaders routinely hide behind their "lesser". I just don't take jobs in the Cluster. Everyone knows it, those who know I exist at least. The Cluster is not a challenge. I don't say that with a sense of arrogance, it is just that the Cluster is incapable of resisting the more powerful members of SA society. It would be like being proud of ripping a kite out of a child's hand. Their shields don't work against our magic, they have no security protocols to block shadows from entering a room, they don't even believe that the SA uses real magic. I have never told Irate this, but all the missions I had gotten from him over the years, I gave to initiates. I use the Cluster to train the fresh faces I don't want to see nabbed by authorities their first assignment. To be frank, the tasks do not even pay well enough to justify operating here. That being said, Irate has always thought the profit to be great and the risks to be greater, an illusion of his I have not cared to break.

Seeing I was not having anything of it he broke the silence with "It is very well paid, even by your guild's prices."

I laughed.

He scowled.

I covered my laugh by striding straight into my response. "I… don't think you can afford my service. I know you are a very wealthy man, but you know we SA are finicky with how we get paid. Your credits mean little to me, and though I value our… friendship…" I hid a sigh "It is just simply impossible for you to have goods I would be interested in." And by goods I meant magical relics. In my position that is exactly what I get paid in. That and power, real, ancient Terran power. But none of that existed outside the SA.

"Lagard, I am desperate, and more importantly you will want to take this if you hear me out."

I began standing up, pocketing the chip. I felt like extending the conversation would only harm my fragile alliance. Where this conversation was going would only be insulting to this proud crime lord. I stood and turned to him to wish him the best. I sensed movement and as I turned to him, he had managed to pull something out of his pocket with a speed even I found impressive. Do not underestimate Clusterites. He could just as easily have had a weapon out, and without my shield on, it would have ended my day regardless of my power level. Luckily, he had not pulled out a weapon. In his hand was a small crystal. He tossed it to me and as I caught it. I could instantly feel the power within it. It looked like a natural grown jagged crystal but it faintly glowed a dark blue. It felt a little warm in my hand and was quite heavy for the size. It was only about six centimeters wide but I found it difficult to hold onto for some reason. As if my body was rejecting the touch of this thing and my instinct kept trying to get me to drop it.

I fell back into my seat. I knew exactly what this was. I was emotionally shocked into feeling weak, which is a rare occurrence for me I assure you. I dropped it into my lap and just stared at it. It was solid state mana but nothing like I had seen in person. Solid state mana came in many forms. The vast majority came in bricks that felt more like wood than crystal. Mana bricks came in all shapes and sizes for whatever devices they were used for, but they all felt the same because they all had the same density of mana. For more demanding devices higher purity forms of mana were produced. Each level of density had its own unique look and feel, but there were only a few levels, making it easy to recognize how pure a block was. As they increased in density, they tended to look more and more jewel like, but at a certain point, at its most pure, the chaotic energies within mana could not be contained and the crystals formed violent shards. This crystal called a Capitol Crystal. It was called so because it was used in high intensity devices that were only found on capitol ships or bases. Zero station for example uses these to deal with the absurdly intense energy cost of opening a gate. Zero station likely has twelve of these connected for any given jump but performs multiple gate openings before exchanging them.

I looked over at Irate, still reeling from the implications and the new questions popping into my head. How had this Cluster kingpin gotten his hands on something even scum like me wouldn't try to steal? What was he using it for? Did he know that this crystal contained magic itself?

"Where the Hell did you get it?!?" I asked in a direct fashion, and in likely a less calm manner than I had intended.

He scowled, clearly offended "I am not some simpleton. You underestimate me Terran."

I sighed, "Fine, you got it somehow and won't elaborate. Now tell me WHY you have it and who is profiting off of this?"

"Your target, my rival."

"Explain. Now." I said firmly but respectfully… I think.

"I am just a middleman." The Fex explained. "I had a… friend… like you. He ran and still runs the Graytin Syndicate. Good man, named Buret Latal. He is a Jans who is devoid of the fuss or stuck up nature that his kind usually exhibit. His grounded manners and attitude got him pretty far in the Wildlands. He was half pirate, half labor manager. He had always been curious about the SA but after some failed attempts to capture SA citizens, his interest in the SA became obsessive. He was convinced your kind held mythical powers, which was fed by his superstitious nature. Buret began seeking people in the SA underground to acquire information and relics from your people. He often spoke to me about how frustratingly little your people gave, even your hardened criminals. One day he excitingly explained to me how he was approached by a mysterious traveler from your society who offered him an item of some kind. The item was some sort of pendant, though I don't know why any pendant would be worth all that trouble."

This concerned me. Irate didn't know this but pendants as a magical item were good at binding Soul and Life magic. It had something to do with the pendant being close to the heart. Magical pendants could mean almost anything in that range, from enhancing the emotional memories of a past love, to giving magically boosted physical capabilities.

Point is, they are mostly the sorts of magic that someone who knows nothing about magic could still use.

Irate continued the story. "He went out of communication for a while, maybe about a month. The only way I knew he had resurfaced was because another syndicate leader was complaining to me about him. Buret used to be competent, but somewhat compliant, making him a threat to no one. He was now throwing his weight around it seemed, and making headway to boot. He muscled in on some territory and started running aggressive hits on opponents. He was quite successful at it employing expensive hitters, which made him number one enemy. He burned bridges with everyone, and frankly politically fucked himself. No one would do business with him which is why when he approached me, it was from a point of desperation. I felt inclined to help him for our past relationship. What can I say, I am sentimental."

I guessed "You mean he paid you really well."
Irate smiled, "A grotesque amount."

"I take it, he paid you to acquire these crystals?"

"Good guess, but not quite. Like I said, I was just the middleman. He had some connection that acquired the crystals. My couriers would pick them up at the edge of the Wildlands and deliver them first here on Nexus to me, then to some final destination through courier. It seemed that his ability to do business in the Wildlands had been diminished during his recent fights."

Who was this guy? What sort of contact would he have that would deliver Capitol Crystals? These crystals were only made on Oceana and each one was heavily accounted for and controlled. That would require some very serious, heavy influence in the SA or a thief more masterful than I was. How could this random Cluster thug get such contacts? "So why do you need me? Sounds like you are still doing business with this scumbag."

Irate responded "I was. The deliveries in the Wildlands stopped. I am assuming his contact in the SA has failed, a testament to your people's security no doubt. When I stopped delivering, he blamed me and began targeting my people as some sort of punishment. Given how violent and abnormal his behavior has been as of late, it did not come as a complete surprise. I am more concerned that he is succeeding."

I had to ask at this point "How many of these crystals did this guy get before he was cut off?"

"Well…" Irate seemed almost nervous to answer that question. "It has been a few months now, and I delivered… let's think…"

"How many!?" I asked in an increasingly irritated tone.

Irate glared at me "26"

"God Almighty" I spat out of both as a curse and a legitimate plea. "Do you know what you have done Irate? I … " All I could think about was how much these things were worth to the SA underground. Hell, how valuable they were to the SA on a whole, but it wasn't worth that to the Cluster. To the Cluster they were a weird source of energy, like really expensive batteries to devices they didn't own. I did not want Irate to know how valuable the merchandise was that had passed through his hands. He was staring at me at this point. So I continued, "I… think that these items are very dangerous." Not a lie. I was quite upset at a Cluster member for having them.

"Yes, but I transport dangerous goods all the time. My whole business is danger, don't forget."

I scoffed at this since he knew not of what he spoke and asked "So where do I come in?

"According to my informants Buret has some sort of dependency on the crystals, and likely has extended use for them, like reserving drugs for an addiction. He has supposedly a year's supply at this point. He gets something from them, and if they were stolen, he would suffer greatly and perhaps lose the mysterious advantage he has over the rest of us."

"Well that would explain why he got so upset when the shipments stopped." I was pretty convinced at this point that this Cluster crime lord was drawing on the crystals for some magical spell he was using against his competitors. Without it, he was probably dead meat with how many enemies he had created.

Irate finished his proposal with "Now that you know the full of it, will you take the job? I will pay more than you might expect, just ask for what you want, and see what I say."

"Irate, you have nothing material that would pay my price. I will take the job though, for the price of an unrestricted favor."

"Is that all?" The naïve Fex asked. "Why that is easy, I will give you three favors for this job!"

I was surprised by this. Even after all the work we did together Irate still didn't understand the significance a favor held when made with a Terran. I couldn't help but smile from ear to ear, which I think unsettled Irate a bit. I agreed to the deal and we shook on it in the standard way, with blood. He had not expected that but obliged my "superstitious cultural oddities" as he put it.

After the deal was made to eliminate his opponent, we went over some details of the job. First and foremost was that Buret couldn't be found. My slippery target had become annoyingly paranoid and Irate had no personal item of his for me to track him with. Just to ship the crystals to Buret, Irate had to send agents… one way. Let's just say, his couriers were associates of Irate that had fallen out of favor. Their fates were not known, but could be guessed. No one alive knew where Buret was, and unfortunately, I had no body to speak to either.

Irate had this issue solved though. He had one crystal remaining that he had reserved when the SA side of the delivery network went dark. Irate would schedule another courier to send the crystal onto Buret, this time as a false peace offering. My task was to follow the courier completely undetected for an indefinite amount of time as the courier traveled from relay to relay, finally being given his last set of coordinates to deliver the crystal. This would be no easy task, even by my standards. Irate and I had no doubt the courier would be watched for at least the last part of the trip to see if he was being followed and likely would have to switch between both private and public transports. I could use an SA disguise kit, but I had a feeling that if my target was a wise to the SA as I thought he was, he would use well known techniques to spot disguised trackers that he would then use to guide me into a trap. Either way, in a few days I would be following the courier from a starting point on Nexus.

When I got to my target, I would need to steal the crystals back. Irate had no idea how much they were worth in the SA underground and I would pocket a huge win for my guild. The loot would be worth more than a hundred favors from Irate, plus the Cluster was finally offering a challenge that interested me. I was taking this job one way or another.

We wrapped up are meeting and Irate picked up his drink. He made a toast to the SA. "I hear it is your year 2000. Usually superstitious races mark millennia with fear and apprehension about 'The End'. Congratulations on surviving." He smiled at his own joke. And it was a joke. He was like many in the Cluster who thought SA citizens were primitively superstitious, but he was also just poking fun at the concept in general. As I stood up to leave, pocketing the Capitol Crystal, I with all sincerity said "Oh that is silly Irate, that doesn't happen until 2050." He could never tell when I was joking or not, so he awkwardly laughed. As I walked out, I knew I had a job to do. I was getting paid a tremendous amount to end Irate's rival. *Oh Damn* I realized I was sort of hired to end the threat in general, plus there was no sense in someone who owes me favors dying. I turned right before leaving and said "Irate, I would consider getting someone else to serve you drinks." He got the hint after a short moment of confusion and hesitation and a look of anger crossed his face. I walked out of the booth and then the tavern. I was headed straight to the headquarters of my guild's Cluster operations.

"You have to do what!?" The confused Elf examined me as if trying to figure out whether I had just lost my mind. He did that really well. Enel the Adept didn't get his name by accident. He was a skilled Elf artisan trained in the ways of the Old Republic. It is no wonder, he was over a century old before the Rec Wars upheaved his society and the old ways were exposed to the new.

He was the sort of man that wore his class out in the open, and people were left the impression that he was pompous. I am pretty sure he isn't, that his attitude purposely distanced people, but I never figured out why. I am not much of a people person though. I just knew to respect him, at least as much as I tend to show. Like I said, I am not good with people, and usually terrible with stuffy people.

I responded, "You heard me Enel. I am not fond of the idea either, but I see no other way. I am a professional though, and I have put myself in more uncomfortable positions before."

"Hmm. Well I will make the suit as comfortable as possible."

That meant something to me, when The Adept said he would make something comfortable, that was an understatement. He had made furniture as well as many other luxury items from Praetors to Emperors alike over the centuries and they all loved his work.

Enel looked down at some papers and began performing some calculations with a fountain pen. All by hand and in his head... old school indeed. He spoke after some scribbling "I can get the suit to sustain you for six months, 2 weeks, and a little over 3 days. That is a prototype of course, and future versions will likely have run times in the years."

I winced at the thought of that. "I only need it for a few weeks, but thanks." Three weeks sealed in a suit... I saw no other way. I needed to stalk a target as he went from relay to relay, completely undetected. The only way I felt safe doing that was to stalk in an extremely stealthy manner. Enel was already drawing up designs for a suit that, once sealed in it, I would not leave it, even for a moment, for an indefinite amount of time. The suit would run my metabolic processes, process my body's needs, sustain my nutrients, and allow me to feel rested with only a couple of hours a sleep at night. It would block my life energy, shield me visually, dampen sounds I made, and except for allowing me to walk through bulkheads make me effectively a ghost.

"Hey, why can't it do that too." Enel looked up at me confused. *Oh I didn't say that last one out loud.* "Why can't the suit allow me to walk though objects and walls?"

He glanced back down to his papers as if not wishing to waste the time looking at me as he answered something so obvious. "If on a ship, you would be a little tied to the mass around you, but if your ship accelerates... Well let's just say the term 'man overboard' comes to mind."

Eesh. Talk about a slow death, my suit would keep me alive for months as I floated through empty space. "Ok, just build the damned thing and I will just take it from there."

Enel looked up and asked, "Why don't you just use your tattoo instead of going through all this effort. You are known as the 'Unseen' Are you not?"

"I am stepping up my game. Plus, I want to overestimate my target. There is something about this guy that has me worried."

The honored Elf nodded. "Wise... for your age." He had a bit of a smile, which made me laugh. Since he had come to work for me, I grew to enjoy his company. Don't get me wrong, we had never bonded as friends do, but we greatly respected each other's abilities. His was to create items as powerful and complicated as they were beautiful. Mine was, and is, to stay alive while doing things I shouldn't be doing.

I honestly have no idea why he did come to work for me. He was an honored member of SA society. I didn't know many details of his life, but what I did know did not scream criminal. He none the less sought me out in the 1990s and I gladly accepted his help. I have never understood his motivations, with the only thing he has ever said in that regard was that my guild offered him "unique problems".

Enel spoke, "I will include pocket of holding, and a special area for your construct." Spark was the name of my construct, and unlike me, he was truly the 'Unseen', or perhaps the Unknown. Everyone thought he was an electronic construct as he hid in devices that looked like would house such a thing. He was however an air elemental. He was an absolute whiz at computers though, and at extracting codes from people. He had tricked everyone into thinking he was a non-sentient AI, even taking the name Spark, and he insisted me taking the credit for choosing the name. I liked that he kept his identity secret, it made him my secret weapon, but I could never figure out why he kept his identity as a sentient so closely guarded. He only ever told me that "Old Friends" would catch up.

I am telling you this, this deepest of secrets because almost a year ago Spark left my company in a hurry and I have not seen from him since. I don't know where he is but there is no harm in releasing his secret, and perhaps the information getting out there may lead someone to helping him. My current worries aside, back to the tale.

I spoke to Enel, "I leave in three days, so I will need this quick"

This elicited a look from the Elf indicating I had become tiresome and said something I have heard out of him a hundred times "I will not be put..."

I interrupted him this time and finished his sentence. He hated that "...on a schedule" I looked at him flatly.

He glared at me in a way only someone from the Old Republic could. Whoever might be reading this, I swear to you now, with all the generations of Elves that have grown up since 1650, even in The Republic now, when Enel's generation goes, that glare will go with them.

"Well Enel, then you aren't going to like what I am going to ask next. On top of the suit, I need you to make a couple a dozen fake Capitol Crystals. They don't need to be fancy, just have a bit of mana in them for show."

"You are not paying me enough gold for this." Enel responded.

"I don't pay you at all." I smiled. Enel often used terms from a long-ago age when currency still existed on Earth. He did receive material compensation from our jobs however, usually in the form of magic item components.

I had three days until I was on my long-term stalking mission, and I wanted nothing more than to spend them doing some last-minute fun or relaxation. Instead I did some last-minute paperwork before I handed my guild over to my second. The glorious life of a leader...

Enel was right, he did make the suit comfortable. I stood in the grungy ally smelling… lilacs? *Damn Enel, you do pay attention to detail.* The master craftsman and artifice had incorporated a day/night air system that fed me different environments. I would say smells, but it wasn't just that. It absolutely felt as though I were standing in a field of flowers with a cool comforting breeze washing over me. The smells, temperatures, and air would change depending on both the time of day and my comfort level.

As promised the suit had a pocket of holding, in which laid several of my favorite thieving devices. It held a simple SA assassin's blade (In case of emergencies), a box full of fake crystals, a lock and trap scanner, an illusion kit, medical supplies, a wall cutter that doubled as a ranged weapon, and of course a whole suite of tools to get me past locks. The crystals were an amazing replica, far better than I had expected. They were fine enough replicas for me to worry about losing track of which were real and which were fake, so I returned the genuine crystal to Irate a few hours previous with a label I had stuck on it reading "real one". These fakes hummed with the same kind of power that the real ones did, though were made with orders of magnitude less mana. Additionally, Enel booby trapped them a what is commonly called a "Malagon Surprise" or what Dwarven strategists still traditionally call "Black Gate Gifting". Basically, sometime after I would leave the fake crystals, hopefully long after, Buret would get a nasty shock when he used them. It wouldn't blow up in his face or anything, but it wouldn't be pleasant either, likely making him sick for some time. It was sort of petty, but I had a feeling Enel was agitated that this Cluster scum had powerful SA resources.

After three days of nearly sleepless work from Enel and days of mind-numbing paperwork from me I was finally stalking my target. I stood in an alley watching a pathetic wretch of a creature. He was a Manuk, one of the species subjugated by the Jans. Between his gaunt features, slouched posture, and glazed look it was obvious to me he had spent years drowned in narcotics. Before you get all touchy feely about the poor Cluster races and their addictive drugs, yes they have plenty of them, yes many drugs in the Cluster are trash, designed to keep people hooked, but these people get a lot of offers of help. If you are drugged up, and no one is forcing you to be so, there is no excuse, even in the Cluster. Cluster doctors can easily purge street drugs from people's systems with next to no chance of continuing physiological dependence.

I sensed a presence I had known for years swoop into the alley and dart into my suit. It spoke to me with a clear voice in my head "Lagard, your target is an idiot."

"Spark, have some respect."

"No Lagard, not this time. Even averaging to my normal lack of respect for flesh bound sentients, this man is an idiot. No wonder Irate wants to get rid of him, I want to at this point."

I sighed. The little air elemental did not tolerate incompetence or frailties. It certainly was not because he didn't have any himself, but his were... different than most other people's. "What did you find out?"

"His name is Bo."

"Yes, I know that already."

"So impatient! I wanted to make sure Irate was not lying to us as to who we were following. I also found out this low life's life story. He joined up with a gang running out of Jans territory when he was young after his family was sold into slavery by the Jans."

I sighed again. Brutal and primitive place the Cluster was. "That is a shame."

Spark paused as if considering that it was possibly a shame for the first time. "Is it? I will have to take your word for it. Continuing on... our target has since lived as scum, being both abused and abuser alike. He is too petty and short sighted to move above errand boy or low-level dealer, no matter the organization he joins. Since he has joined Irate's crew, he has only trashed his chances further. He provokes fights, steals merchandise, and most recently tried an awkwardly complicated and faulty scheme to embezzle Irate out of his cut."

"Well, I can see why he was picked for this mission."

"I wouldn't even bother with this show, why doesn't Irate just throw him in a bottomless pit and just use a droid as a courier."

"Droids can get highjacked, and Irate doesn't know for certain what Bo's fate will be, so he may not want him dead straight out. Plus, crime lords here don't have bottomless pits."

Spark paused and responded "Now THAT is a shame, but also a good point… about the bottomless pit I mean. The rest is garbage. We both know this guy will end up dead and the only one who doesn't know it is Bo."

"Fine, let's just get to this then, he is being called into Irate's place now."

I followed Bo into Irate's headquarters, which I had never seen before. It was simple, surprisingly so. No show, no fuss, purely utilitarian. I was surprised. I guess Irate saves the royal crime lord routine for his business partners and clients.

I followed Bo closely, avoiding bumping into him and his escorts. It got awkward once we entered a lift together, but thanks to a wall climb feature of the suit, I just crawled up one of the walls and stayed on the ceiling to avoid any problems. The deeper parts of the headquarters had some of Irate's personal wealth displayed, but not much. I firmly ordered Spark to not steal a thing. Yes, I have had to be quite insistent at times to keep him from stealing. One of his glaring weaknesses was the inability to stop himself from stealing. I have no idea where items went when he grabbed them, the term 'disappearing into thin air' comes to mind, but Spark has only ever said about it is that things end up in his 'pockets'. Whatever that meant, I did not want him to pocket anything here. Irate knew we were tailing Bo as well as my general capacity to go unnoticed. Irate would rightfully assume I had stolen something from his HQ.

After some conversation between Irate and Bo, Irate handed his ill-fated courier the last Capitol Crystal and a computer pad used by Buret to message the couriers saying "Succeed at this mission, and all will be forgiven." With a wicked smile on his face, Bo bowed and exited Irate's office. We left Irate's office, following our target to a local port.

Bo had a surprisingly self-assured stride as he went, as if he had just gotten away with murder. Spark pipped up "Arrogant moron, let's just kill him here and take his place."

"Spark! We will do no such thing. I will not slay this person for no reason, and frankly that would be a very sloppy way to carry this mission out. Why do you have to always jump to the violent solution?"

"I don't!" Spark objected. "I just think pragmatically."

"Oh really…" I shot back "Is that why last week you lobbied me to flog initiates that screwed up on missions?"

"Exactly my point" Spark responded as if he had just won the argument. "I had not even considered that idea until you turned down my fire and ice idea."

"Spark, sometimes with your respect for 'mortals', I wonder why you are not working for one of the assassin guilds instead."

"Who is to say I am not…?" Spark paused after saying this. That was something I had never considered, that he could be working for two guilds. It wasn't unheard of, there was no exclusion clause in our guild. I just never thought of my little kleptomaniac friend running around on kill missions while I was catching up on guild paperwork. Spark continued now with a surprisingly thoughtful tone. "It's not that I don't respect fleshy mortals. I mean I think you are decent enough of a fellow and you are as fleshy as they come."

"…Thanks?"

"You're welcome. My point is that I think you underestimate my respect whenever I suggest murder stabbing." I paused, genuinely confused where Spark was going with this. He continued "I subscribe to what the dragons think. That you mortals live such short and often seemingly wasteful lives, because you have so many to give. I really believe… no, I KNOW, you have many lives to give and your soul will bounce from fleshy living corpse to fleshy living corpse every time you die. Unlike the Drago though, I don't consider it a weakness, but a strength. So, if you absolutely believed that your kind respawned every time you died, and that my kind only had one life, one continuous experience to give, why wouldn't you kill you all by the bunches? It seems a lot nicer than letting some dimwit carry on in a clearly failed life, when you can sort of reset them and hope for a better outcome."

His logic was so warped, yet sort of made sense. I mean, from his perspective murder was a … blessing? God, I hope, wherever he is now he is not running around in charge of an assassin's guild, because I am pretty sure they would be gleefully handing out murders like it was a candy.

We went on silent after that, just listening to conversations, and watching our target as he waited at the port. After an hour Bo looked at his pad as if something had gotten his attention on it, then turned and walked over to an empty kiosk. He reached behind it and pulled out something that had been affixed to the bottom of the counter. It was a transport pass for a ship that was scheduled to leave in just a few minutes. He shoved it in his pocket and hurried to the appropriate boarding hanger. We kept up with him, even as the crowds got thick, making it difficult to pass without bumping into someone. It was always a lot harder to avoid people when they didn't know you were there, but I was quite used to this concept already. It was easy to follow Bo even though he barely made it to the transport in time.

It appeared that whoever was feeding him instructions did not want Bo to know his own travel plans until the last moment. This was a pattern that would be followed throughout our journey. Every place we ended up in, it was rarely obvious where, when, or by what means the next destination would be reached. It seemed almost random at times, but there was a logic to it. By keeping Bo running from place to place, it made it harder for either Irate's agents, or local authorities to keep watch of Bo without making it obvious they were indeed following him.

This technique became tiresome rather quickly though and I could tell Bo's stress levels were increasing. Bo responded to the stress in what seemed to be a typical pattern for him. At first it was just extra drinks, then it was harder drugs, and finally it was staying up all night without sleeping. Bo was not just being worn down by Buret, but wearing himself down. After a few weeks of traveling like this, it was becoming obvious to Spark and I that Bo was about to do something stupid.

We were on our eighth public transport in a fine dining area. This transport was a bit nicer than the others, not as nice as the three private shuttle services we took, but definitely better than the five cargo ships we stowed away on. We had been it seemed all over this part of the Cluster, from Chaos territory to the Garn homeworld, and now were heading back through Middle Alliance territory. Bo should have been spending this leg of the trip, which was probably the longest being four days in total, resting and enjoying some nice meals. Bo had had instead spent the previous night trying to find a buyer on the ship for more of his drugs. He had not had time at our last stop to get more narcotics by the time we had to rush over to ship we were on now.

He was sitting at the bar, drinking more than enough for a Cluster species to become belligerent when an attractive Braxin woman sat next to him. She wore clothes that suggested she had lived in the Middle Alliance for some years, and between her bound blond hair, her posture, and her boots, it was obvious she was off duty Middle Alliance military. After watching Bo for far too long, which included staying in his quarters while he slept, I knew him too well to think this was going to go well. Spark recognized it too, and I could feel him perk up in excitement. For an elemental he was remarkably restless. Perhaps air elementals were more fidgety than earth ones, but all I knew was that Spark was getting very bored, and now he sensed entertainment.

As if on que, Bo swiveled in his chair, gave a creepy look up and down the Braxin woman, and said something that was so ridiculously idiotic, it took even me by surprise. "Those clothes look tight on you. You want help taking them off?"

I was impressed how fast the woman's response was. Not necessarily the physical speed, but how fast this woman emotionally went from relaxed and safe social environment to full on violence. Without pause she stopped reaching for a drink in front of her she had just been served, swung her arm around and smacked Bo so hard he fell backwards off his chair and straight onto the ground.

This got the room to react and everyone turned to this spectacle, all except three. Bo and the woman had more exchanges, and Bo even tried to strike her, though that did not end well for him. While Spark and everyone else was paying attention to the fight, I was watching the three who were not reacting. This was a great opportunity and I was going to take it. There was about a 98% chance one of these three were and agent of Buret, here to watch Bo, and it was obvious to me which one it was. I recognized all three. One was a Braxin bruiser and murderer who was recently taking refuge employed in small Hizarin mercenary company. The second was a Volkris thief that specialized in corporate espionage. He was working in Garn territory as a freelancer these days and made quite a bit of wealth staying away from waring crime lords. The third was a former Garn investigator named Emin that ran advanced interrogation techniques for the underground organizations. He was very good at his job and fetched a hefty price for his services. Whoever had hired him had wealth and connections, perfect fit for Buret.

Some security came in at this point and though Buret's agent stayed, the other two criminals made graceful exits. Security dragged Bo away and I followed. The ship had a very light amount of security, but it was better than nothing. They scanned Bo and the ship's surgeon gave him something to calm down. I stayed with Bo as he slept... again, and the ship's captain announced there would be an unscheduled detour to Nexus. It had nothing to do with Bo it seemed, throwing him off the ship was just a bonus for the captain. I was curious so asked Spark to investigate the detour while I watched Bo.

When Spark returned, he reported that the ship captain had received orders from their transport company's stop coordinator to change their schedule and make a stop on Nexus immediately. *Slick* I thought. Buret was obviously VERY well connected, and had this transport make a detour just to shake off anyone tracking Bo from afar. At least, that is what I was guessing.

It became obvious I was correct shortly after we disembarked the transport on Nexus. Bo was awake now and a bit calmer having drugs purged out of his system and his physiology stabilized. He was dumped onto port security whom, after finding several warrants were out for his arrest, made plans to hand him over to Nexus police. Bo was looking nervous again and his posture became more hunched as we waited for the local police to be called. The port security Chief was an aged and overweight Fex. He sat behind his desk filling out some final paperwork, being a man who clearly followed bureaucratic rules even if they slowed him down. That is when Emin entered, escorted by one of the port security.

The Garn addressed the chief respectfully and followed protocol precisely, asking for Bo to be handed over to Emin. The chief explained that while handing over a belligerent and clearly troubled passenger to a civilian next of kin or friend was normally acceptable to the rules, Bo had outstanding warrants that made it a Middle Alliance security matter. Emin asked for a private audience with the Chief, who granted his request, and both Bo and the other security agents were kicked out of the chief's office. It was only a few minutes, and according to Spark it was a rather boring conversation, but Bo was released into Emin's custody and his records of arrival were stricken due to "misidentification" of the passenger.

Bo walked out of the port with Emin switching from his craven look back to his oh so confident stride. Bo had gotten away once again, due to his massive connections. I distinctively remember thinking *Boy, maybe Spark had the right idea after all.*

It didn't take long to realize that Buret was on Nexus. This was the final destination after all, and the last few weeks were all a smoke screen. After about twenty minutes in a ground vehicle (locals colloquially call them cars apparently referring back to some machine version of a carriage) we arrived in an abandoned industrial area. The place looked like it used to be a place where companies could rent multileveled factories and use on site systems and machinery, but the owners had long gone bankrupt leaving the land to rot. It was one of those parts of Nexus that Terrans just plain hated. All pipes, roads, and hangers, even Dwarven industrial cities would have far more art and life in it. It was very empty though, which is was a nice change of pace.

We got out of the vehicle and proceeded into one of the abandoned factories. I could feel us being watched though to the watcher's credit I could not spot them outright. We wove in and out of catwalks and broken pipes until we reached a large industrial elevator. About twenty by twenty meters, it was far too large for individuals to regularly take, but likely this was the only way into Buret's base. Emin and his now four security all stood around the now smug and worriless Bo and the elevator lurched to life. We moved down and as we did, we could see exposed metal frames and dark factory floors. The scenery was like this for a few moments until the abandoned rooms gave way to solid metal walls. It was obvious that we were traveling deep within Nexus itself. I have some very detailed maps on Nexus, but there are many layers just lost to time. This was one of them. Kilometers below the surface sat geothermal collectors, forges, and antimatter power generators. It gave Nexus a layered city feel that was unmatched in SA territory. I think the Dwarves again come the closest, perhaps the Goblins coming close as well, but even then, they never had a population large enough or stupid enough to live in the mega-slums.

After a few minutes, 2.4 km down if my calculations were correct, we stopped. In front of us were a pair of doors that stood out from the rest of the environment. These looked like they used to be large industrial hanger doors, but something had been altered on them. They had lines and patterns, nothing complex, nothing too artistic, that made it look somehow more ornate. Without ceremony or a word from Emin the doors opened. What we entered was so contrary to the surface, or anything I had seen on Nexus, I found it impressive. Inside was nothing short of a spacious palace, filled with expensive decorations, comfortable seating, fountains of alcohol, and hurried servants. Multiple agents of Buret were lounging, talking, and eating. It seemed like a party of sorts, but that was like comparing a wood fire to smoldering coal. It appeared, much contrary to how Irate ran his organization, that Buret's people were in a constant state of luxurious pleasure. It became clear that the servants were indeed slaves, and that male and female alike they were there at the complete whim of Buret's people.

The architecture was the weirdest part. I couldn't put my finger on it but there was something familiar about it. If it were not on Nexus, I would have guessed it to be a weird combination of super Old Republic Elven and Gothic Human. In a strange way, the shapes and angles of the walls seemed to encourage shadows.

Bo took the scene in and mistakenly, yet again, thought he had made it big. Emin gestured to a female servant who shuffled over. A tray of drinks was held out for Bo and the sniveling scum took his time to pick. He grabbed the largest looking drink and winked at the servant who returned the look with a blank glazed stare… *God are the servants drugged?!* I wondered. This look however was apparently all the encouragement Bo needed to creepily smile back.

Bo spoke. "Mr… Err… Amin is it? Please direct me to Buret, I want to get business done so I can join the party."

Emin said "Of course, right this way."

As we moved into a quieter part of the palace Spark piped up. "God these are my sort of people!"

I scowled, which in retrospect was a useless exercise to do when having a conversation with an invisible entitee hiding in your pocket. "Spark, what the Hell are you talking about?"

"Isn't it obvious? These people, all these wonderful people, I could rob and kill every single one and you would never so much as complain at me for it. Like I said, my favorite sort of people."

I morbidly laughed. He was right, this was the sort of scum I hated, but I had to focus on the mission. "Spark, while I find out where they are taking Bo, I need you to scout around and get a lay of the land."

"Ok! As I do… Can I… Do I….?"

I knew what he was trying to ask. He wanted to know how subtle he had to be. If I wanted to expertly perform this mission it required stealth and skill, it required subterfuge and information gathering. It had required me to intimately sit with Bo for over three weeks and now put up with sneaking though a scum den… *Fuck It.*

"Don't hurt the servants, rob this place blind."

"Yay!" Spark yelled with excitement though I was still the only one who could hear him. He exited his housing in the suit and literally breezed down a perpendicular hallway. The little guy was funny. He could squeeze down to a dense mouse size or expand up to a human size depending on what he needed. Either way, he was virtually invisible if he wished, or could appear as cloud and fog. In this case he expanded to human sized, staying completely see through, and traveled as a strong wind to an adjacent part of the palace.

As he traveled down the hall anything loose, including displayed wealth and tapestries rattled and wobbled. A vase tipped over and simply... disappeared. No matter how many times I have seen Spark frob something, it never got old. He passed by them and they vanished, quite literally into thin air. A painting ripped off the wall in the wind and never made it to the ground. A display case popped open in the breeze and a grotesquely ornate necklace was sucked up into nothing as if hit by a tornado. By the time the hallway had calmed down, and Spark was out of sight, it was virtually empty. Only the rug and empty displays remained. I remember thinking at that moment *There is no going back now. At least I don't need to do a crystal swap, I will just grab them and run.*

I caught up to Bo and company to find the wretch being escorted into a room with a thick door and even thicker walls. The door was opened and inside was a single chair in the center of the room. This was not looking good for Bo at this point, but he kept pressing on as if he were about to be rewarded. "Give me the crystal and sit." Emin said. His voice had changed from a calm tone to something more commanding and intimidating.

"I can't." Bo said, his voice beginning to shake and his posture reentering its hunched position. "I have to give this directly to Buret"

"Trust me" Emin said with a deep smooth rumble. At this Bo pulled out the crystal and handed it to Emin. Emin examined it with some sort of electronic device, made an approving grunt, and turned to look down the hall. At that moment a Hizarin woman walked out of an adjacent room with a Hizarin male trailing behind her. She walked up to

Emin and he handed her the Crystal saying, "Take this to the Lord while I debrief our guest."

The Hizarin female took the crystal but immediately turned to the male following her and shoved it violently into his chest forcing him to grab onto it. She said with a viciously sharp hiss "Drop this bug, and I will gut you."

Wow I thought, but the surprise was not great on my part, as I had immediately recognized her, not by her look, but by her voice. She was a vindictive bounty hunter wanted by the Hizarin government for assassinating a general a couple of years back. She had a reputation for absurdly impractical violence, and psychologically playing with her targets before killing them. There was no official image of her, well until now as I was making a full scan of her, but her voice I had heard in some transmissions that crossed my desk about a year ago. No one knew her name, but the Huntsman guild named her Raptor.

Damn I thought. This is high cost help. I knew Emin was pricy as well, and there were a few other expensive faces I noticed after entering the main entrance. It was a traditional Cluster crime lord tactic to have a large body of indebted low lives with a few outside hired hitters. Buret on the other hand seemed to rely heavily on high class goons. This likely limited his ability to do business on the streets, but it would give him a great ability to war with other organizations. This would make it more difficult for me if things went south. I was now surrounded by competent help of whom a great many of them had already gotten over SA shock. They likely would be prepared for classic Terran tricks.

I followed the Hizarins for minutes before we reached nearly the other side of the palace. We entered what appeared to be an antechamber set up for meditation. There were candles set up everywhere, a rarity in the cluster, and large patterned rug on the ground. Kneeling in the center was a cloaked figure who did not move from his spot, but spoke. "You have it, bring it here." Raptor shoved her slave over to the cloaked figure and the servant quickly placed the crystal down in front of the supposed Lord. The cloaked figure, presumably Buret, reached his hand out and felt the crystal. This was strange for a person from the Cluster. He was not using a tool to scan the crystal but seemed to be feeling it with senses unknown to Cluster races.

The cloaked figure pulled back his hand and said "Excellent, take it into the Chamber. I wish to use it before placing it with the others." This was good news for me. It meant all the crystals were in one place and I would soon be shown where. Raptor said "Take it in" to her slave and as he carried out his orders, I heard a voice pop up in my head. Spark was speaking to me. We had a magical link set up years ago that allowed us to communicate by thoughts at distance. Spark said "Good news, I found a security room that takes care of all the electronics of this facility. Additionally, someone is making a call to Buret. The operators here are debating whether to interrupt Buret with the summons."

Before the slave could return from delivering the crystal to the adjoining chamber a voice came into the room over some sort of communication system. "Lord, please excuse the interruption, but you have a transmission coming in specifically for you."

The "lord" still presumably Buret stood saying "How strange, send it to my meditation chamber." As his agents patched the call, without turning he said to Raptor "After Emin is done with Irate's agent, take him to the Chamber and leave him there."

She bowed slightly, said "Yes Master" and made her exit, her servant close behind her. *Master!?* This was not your typical Cluster crime lord. I had a sudden fear that this was not Buret at all, but an SA citizen who had taken his place. I repositioned myself between him and a computer panel he was approaching. As I got closer, he took his cloak off and began pressing at the panel to activate. He was… Jans. *Weird.* I mean it was good news, but seemed like a sharp personality shift from the Buret Irate had described. Granted that is what had shocked the rest of the local crime bosses as well.

The panel lit up and a call was connected. On the other side of the call was another cloaked figure. This one with her cowl covering most of her face. Between the shadows on her end and the cloak I could only see her lips and upper torso. She was what I would normally find quite appealing. The term 'full' came to mind. She had red swollen lips, an exposed swelling chest, and a broad delicate collar bone. Her neck had a choker on it that screamed lady, and fair smooth skin. Again, normally I would have found her quite beautiful, but instead I had a feeling of repulsion. I am emphasizing this part of the story because of how strange it was. The contradiction of feelings made me feel sick and unsettled. There was something deeply wrong with how she looked. I don't know if it was because her skin was just too fair, almost pale, or the shadows falling on her seemed to almost unnaturally smooth out her features.

When she spoke it came out a deep but feminine purr, however in a strangely raspy fashion. "I hear you are out and about."

"No thanks to you treasonous witch" Buret instantly losing his cool in this conversation he spat back.

The not-beauty gave a wicked smile and said "What did you expect? Your insolence was intolerable."

"When the other Kings find out that you have exiled me, a Lord, to this primitive backwash of a region, they will have your head."

She gave a throaty laugh that sounded somehow hollow. "Oh dearie… you just don't get it do you? The others are who pushed me to exile you."

"WHY!?!" This seemed to put Buret into a fit of rage and he pounded the wall with his fists hard enough to bruise or even break hand. He didn't seem to care or notice however and carried out his tantrum anyway.

"Why because you are just not Lord material are you? Your ambition for Kingship hardly endeared you to people either. You are just not made of the right stuff. You are merely a philosopher, a tinkerer, someone who serves greater men.

"I am more than your outdated ways place me, I am power!" He screamed like a child into the wall panel.

"Yes well, in truth, I am here in the Cluster to make sure you were handed over and settled in, but I underestimated your ability to survive. I didn't realize you would find a source of mana to sustain you. I think that is something the rest will look kindly on you for. Perhaps if you make something of yourself here, among the great galactic trash, you will gain our respect in a refreshed manner." *Interesting*, I thought. Somehow Buret needed these crystals to 'sustain' himself. My stealing the crystals would indeed kill or cripple him in some fashion.

Buret, or whatever this creature was, responded "I have grown stronger than you know and will prove it. Soon, you and the others will be begging not only to restate my lordship but to be a fellow King."

More laughter followed by "Surely you do not have a scheme that could take you that far? I await the results future King." She gave a mocking laugh at her own comment and continued. "I don't recommend returning to us looking like that though, you are better off showing up to a royal palace dressed as a rat." She put her lips into a smirk taking the moment to just watch Buret's reaction which was silent rage. She asked, "You must tell me, how did you manage to secure a source of mana out here?"

"I have connections you could not imagine."

"Keep your secrets then, at least tell me what happened to that necklace?"

Buret just fumed for a moment, bringing his temper down before he continued. "I had it destroyed."

She looked sad "Oh that is shame, necklaces like that are so hard to come by. That was petty of you."

Buret's anger seemed to pivot into self-satisfaction at this point and as if he were striking at her with his words, he said "I though, can make another." He strongly emphasized the 'I' in his sentence as if he were capable of doing something she was not. The transmission ended and Buret fell to his knees again, covered his head with his hands... and... wept? Who was this guy!?

Buret collected himself and after a few minutes of stillness Emin entered the antechamber. He spoke respectfully to Buret but you could tell he was not fond of treating someone as a greater. "Master, I have extracted anything relevant to Irate's operations from our guest. I had him placed in the main Chamber."

"Did you find anything useful from this one?"

"Nothing, like most of his couriers they have been distanced from his organization for some time."

"Very good Emin, you have done well."

Emin departed and Buret and I entered the Chamber. It was a half dome chamber in which the domed part was made of thousands of tiny crystal edges. These crystals came from the Cluster and were considered non-magical. That being said, they were worth something to the SA for a reason. They helped focus magical energies for equipment and I suspected in this case as a poor man's Cradle. It was a classic design used by wizards for as many years as magic has existed. It was simple to build, hard to get wrong, and easy to use no matter the magic you pumped through it. One this size, this deep into the planet, it could amplify magic over a massive part of Nexus. Assuming you had the magical energy to do it… *Shit*… The crystals were not just to sustain Buret, but for a spell as I had originally suspected.

The floor was exposed rock that was likely connected to the environment surrounding the palace. On the floor is what disturbed me most. Twenty-six shriveled up corpses were strewn around the floor. They were all in different positions and poses as if laying where they had died. Their bodies looked like they had been placed in a desert for years. They wore clothes matching that of poor cluster syndicate members. Bo lay in a fetal position on the ground muttering to himself. It looked as though he had been in great pain just a few minutes previous and was still recovering.

Buret walked over to him, knelt down, reached for Bo's wrist and guided him up to his knees where they sat eye to eye. "Do not worry courier, you are safe now."

Bo snuffled "I am? Thank you, I told the truth, I hate Irate I gave you everything I have."

"Oh not everything" Buret said. "But soon, I trust you will. I do not question you child, you are forgiven."

People in the cluster keep using that word "forgiven", but I am not sure they know what it means. Buret convinced Bo rather easily that if he knelt and pleaded for his life he would not die and be allowed to stay here in the palace. Buret told Bo exactly what to say, a specific phrase to repeat over and over. For some reason Bo bought it and stammered through the phrase repeating it while staying on his knees.

"Excellent, just like that, don't stop until I say so." Buret said. He walked over to a table on the side of the room that held the Capitol Crystal Bo had brought. Buret took it and placed in at the corner of an elaborate pattern that had been etched into the stone. I took the time to examine it, but had to crawl up the wall to get a full picture. It seemed to me that is was an interwoven pattern that was designed to draw energies from both the crystals and sacrifices with each body placed on a node of some kind. I came back down, my thoughts racing. I was searching my memory for this particular pattern. I was no magic expert, but even I could tell this pattern was both elegant and complex. This was far above anything someone from the cluster could piece together. Hell, I wan't sure if I knew a SA mage capable of this pattern without the complex interweaving energy flow collapsing the spell.

I called Spark and gave him a detailed description. While Spark was taking time to think about my description, I noticed more chanting was picking up in the room, and from other voices other than Bo. They matched the words Bo was saying but every voice was different. They became louder and more in sync with Bo's chanting. I couldn't figure out where the voices were coming from at first. As Buret stood in the center, his arms out, I walked around looking for the source of the voices. It became obvious rather quickly that the voices were not coming from speakers, or even a single source. Each voice was coming from a different shriveled body, or at least the area each corpse laid.

Spark got back to me after some contemplation "I give it a very high likelihood… Well, I know for certain that it is some form of life magic, very old school version at least, but I give it a very high likelihood this is necromancy."

Necromancy!?! "But Spark, the Last Necromancer was called last for a reason. Not to say there is no necromancy, but to say no one has the modernized knowledge to do complicated things like this."

"Oh no, I never said this was modern knowledge. Tyr's stuff would have been considered super new compared to this. Not to say this isn't cutting edge in a sense. It is obvious this is something custom built for the occasion, but whoever put it together sounds like he us using a very old set of rules, like pre-Sealed Kingdom old."

"God almighty, who is this person, what do you think this thing is supposed to do?"

"Well, hang on, let me check their video logs of that room and I will know exactly what they are up to. I just have to get one of the security operators off of his computers."

A moment passed by and I could see the shadows in the room start to warp and twist inward as if they were flowing towards Bo. In the shadows ribbons of lights began to form. Purple and green colors started to wrap around Bo.

"Hey Spark, something is about to happen, I need to stop this NOW."

"Don't! You could get caught in it, and nothing bad is going to happen. For once, follow exactly what I say Lagard."

Spark only ever spoke to me like that when he had information I didn't have and that he knew for all certainty I would act his way if I had it. I froze and let it play through. The ribbons of energy snaked up Bo and seemingly without his notice began... well the only way to describe it was sucking him dry. He didn't act in pain, or even slow down on his chanting. His body simply deformed and dried out, falling to the ground. When I say his chanting didn't slow, I mean it didn't stop. Even after the corpse had landed on the ground I could hear the voice fading but still chanting the same phrase. After a moment the lights returned to normal and the voices in the room subsided.

Buret smiled and walked out of the room, scooping up the Capitol Crystal as we went. I followed and we traveled to an adjacent room empty except a single chest in the middle. I was about to step into the room when Spark once again interrupted me. "Stop" I froze in place half-way stepping into the room. "Don't go in there yet." Spark said. I stepped out and stood by. The door closed and after less than a minute Buret returned, leaving to somewhere else in the Palace.

"Spark, what is going on?"

"OK first, I will need to disable some of the security in the room. His security is much tighter than any other cluster criminal I have seen. You were about to set off both ground and air pressure sensors. You may be undetectable, but you still occupy space, remember? According to the palace AI the room's sensors are tied into the visual inputs, a feature designed specifically to detect invisible people."

"Like the Order of the Black Gate…"
"Yes, this guy is way more prepared than I thought."

I was no longer surprised however, and if it were not for this new puzzle in front of me, I would not have continued to underestimate Buret, if that was his true identity.

"Spark will you be able to disable the room security."

"Yes. The palace AI taught me how to do it. Very helpful little guy. I named him Oochick, the Kolbold word for cute. I also erased him."

"Was that really necessary?"

"Hey, come on, sure he had some personality, but no way was he sentient."

"You sure?" I asked. "From what we can tell this facility has been kicking off magic energy for months and months."

"Arg… fine, let me see if I can retrieve him."

"Are you going to tell me what this ritual is?"

"Right, I examined the footage and it is fascinating stuff. Necromancy designed for a large scale. I mean I have heard about some stuff Tyr did, but he was using the Crystal of Eternal Life, this guy is doing it all with old fashioned blood sacrifices, or mind sacrifices to be exact. Oldie but a Goldie."

"Mind sacrifices?" I asked

"Yeah, I know everyone uses 'blood sacrifice' as an umbrella term, but there are several ways to harvest life energy from mortals. If you need something with a more psychological bent, you can rip someone's mind away at time of death. Unlike blood sacrifices it creates a specter afterwards that you can use for other purposes. Bonus!"

"Spark, how do you know all this stuff? I don't even think the Archmagi knows any of this necromancy stuff, and you are talking about it like you are around it all the time. Are you in any other guilds other than mine?"

The little air elemental laughed. "Really? That is where you are going with this? That I am part of some secret necromantic group? You didn't think that maybe you don't know my past as well as you think you do? I know things, Ok."

Considering I knew nothing of his past, that was saying something. I had not considered that for some reason, but it gave me a chance to poke around his past and, death-defying mission or not, I was not going to lose this opportunity.

"You are right, I don't know your past, but what possible past would intercept you with this stuff?"

Spark sighed, a surprisingly easy feat for a creature made of pure air. "I don't think so."

"What!? You bring it up and don't give any information. I am stopping this mission right now until you tell me."

"Gee, a mortal throwing a tantrum, how original. Keep holding your breath, once you pass out Enel's suit will revive you."

"No Spark, you are not doing this. How the Hell am I supposed to act on information that comes from someone guessing, this information was lost a long time ago and you just can't admit you don't know anything."

"Transparent manipulation Lagard… but fine. I was around. I was around a long time ago and I will not say more, it would put your life at risk."

What!? My life at risk? I was nearly at the top of the SA most wanted, if they knew I existed that is, and knowing Spark's past would be the thing that would get me killed? Who was this little guy, what was he wrapped up in?

"I know Lagard, what you are thinking. Just don't judge. I… have not always been so brazen. There were times… I let people push me around, I was not like the rest, ready to die for no reason. I was sentient damn it and I didn't choose my job!" Wow, Spark was really cracking up over this. I let him continue. "All I will say is that I know this knowledge firsthand and these people second hand. These people are playing for keeps. They may be arrogant, and foolish, but they play very long games. You should have never taken this job."

In all the time I had known Spark this is the first time I knew him to be emotionally down. Shortly before he disappeared a bit ago was the second. He had just been so hopeful about this mission and was suddenly getting fatalistic.

"Spark, snap out of it! Fuck your past, this is the present, and I don't fail. Not with you by my side. Just get back to work. Tell me what this damned spell will do if we don't interfere."

Spark sounding like he was dragging his feet said "It will kill a third of the population of Nexus and instantly turn them into the living dead, enslaved by Buret and controlled by the sacrificed specters acting as his lord generals. In a few days' time Nexus will become a new Kingdom of Eternal life."

"God Almighty… Disable the room's security. I am getting the Capitol Crystals now."

"Done Lagard. Keep in mind though, there are systems that are independent. I will loop the video and fake a few things, but if you trip something on the chest, I will not be able to stop the automatic security measures from engaging."

No more underestimating Buret or whatever the Hell he was. I took my time. It was a full fifteen minutes before I attempted to make it past first lock on the chest. He had them layered, with every kind of Cluster lock imaginable. I had all my tools with me and once I began work each lock only took a moment. No SA lock that I could tell. As I went on to the last layer I paused and rescanned for any subtle magical lock. Nothing. *Ok then… I can just open it…* I opened the chest.

What I didn't know at the time was that a scholar in the SA had created something new. He had invented microscopic glyphs. Even though they now are in many of our devices… and locks, at the time they were virtually unheard of. One such application was for the lowest security devices, storing civilization critical assets, such Capitol Crystals transported, produced, and stored on Oceana.

What I also didn't know at the time was that this chest was not Buret's, or at least not originally. It was stolen from Oceana… I felt a pop. It was not much, but I could tell I tripped something. Something unexpected. I have failed enough times in my life to know that I was not perfect. I had only the briefest moment to act.

It didn't take long at all for the security to spring up. I had managed to get half-way across the room with the chest under my arm when the shield formed all around me. I reached into my tool to grab my wall cutter when a surge of energy hit me. It felt just like a massive water wave smashing into me and while it didn't knock me out it disoriented me greatly. It took me a moment to realize I was on the ground flat on my back.

I didn't waste time. I told my limbs to move but I could only move my right arm. My legs and my left arm were completely pinned by something. I reached to feel if anything physical was pinning me or whether it was a force field. I should have been able to feel something with my right hand, but I felt nothing. That is when I realized I couldn't feel anything, as in I couldn't feel my right hand with my left. My limbs were not pinned, they were numb. The energy discharged had both fried my suit and my nervous system.

I was screwed. There was nothing I could do but lay there and flop around, which I did quite expertly I must say. I tried reaching for my medical supplies to see if I could find something to stimulate or heal my nervous system. I remember thinking as I fumbled *Damn you left arm and legs for not working when my right is fine. Right arm if we get through this, I am giving you a promotion and making you my dominate side.* Weird things go through my head when I am under extreme stress.

I was fiddling with the medical equipment when I noticed people standing over me. I looked toward the ceiling and saw a circle of guns pointed at me. There were five highly trained thugs standing around me. I heard Buret's voice "Get the restraints on him." It seemed redundant to restrain my limbs, but they placed a pair of Fex cuffs on me and my helmet was ripped off. If you have ever been restrained by Fex shackles you will know they are designed for discomfort. They are simple wrist cuffs that have an energy band between them keeping them together at a certain distance, which is with the wrists about 10 cm apart. If the separation distance becomes greater or less by a small margin the wearer gets shocked with an extremely painful plasma charge that runs along your nervous system. It was designed to make a prisoner concentrate so greatly on keeping the cuffs still, that he or she would not be able to fidget out an escape.

I realized that this would work in my favor and as the criminals lifted me, I began shifting my cuffs to cause the plasma charge. I was hoping to stimulate my nerves, though it was quite painful in the non-numb parts of my body. I was held from behind by Raptor and the others held my arms or just pointed guns at me. I was facing Buret who was scowling. "Who sent you?" He asked.

I shot back with as diplomatic of a response as I could manage "If you are too dumb to figure that out, I have no hope for you."

This pissed Buret off but Emin interrupted before Buret could respond. "Irate clearly is behind this. We just took in his agent. Somehow this creature snuck in with him or tracked him."

I heard Raptor speak behind me "Terran savage, you can never predict these primitives"

Buret look furious at me, or I thought it was me at first until I realized he was looking at Raptor. He broke his gaze from Raptor and placed it onto me. "Kill him"

Emin interrupted again and asked "Wait should we not interrogate him? This is a great opportunity my… Lord… A member of the SA could tell us more about their kind. There is no danger in keeping him alive for a day or two for me to…"

Buret raised his hand and Emin went silent. "Emin, you don't know them like I do. He is too dangerous, kill him now before it's too late."

Buret's agents acted stunned. They seemed to be detecting the same nervousness I was getting from Buret, a fear they had never seen in him. Buret knew the SA, for all he knew I was part of an Order of the Black Gate team.

I decided to roll the dice under the hope that Buret's emotional maturity was lower than Spark when it came to detecting transparent manipulation. I put a big smile on and asked "What Buret you worried I am Order of the Black Gate or something?"

He froze though his agents looked confused. I continued. "Don't worry buddy, they wouldn't waste their time on a two-bit Cluster operator."

"Two-bit!?" Buret responded. He gestured to his goons and one of them punched me in the gut.

After I recovered, I started laughing. Borrowing language from the creepy woman he spoke to earlier I said "I heard you were trying a spell or something? I mean for some Cluster trash to be trying to cast a spell, isn't that like a rat trying to write a symphony?" I laughed some more.

Boy did this work. He had his people beat me some more and as they went to shoot me, he stopped them and began dragging me by one of my feet. *Hey,* I thought *I can sort of feel that leg now*. He dragged me into the chamber and spoke to me as he did. "Let me show you what this rat can do!"

After brining me inside the chamber he asked his agents to clear to the edge of the room and placed me on one of the pattern's nodes. He bent down to my ears so that only I could hear. "I am not a Cluster rat, I am a Terran monster." He had Emin bring him the chest and he opened it. He took a moment unlatching one of the 27 crystals in the chest and pulled it out. He paused and squinted his eyes as if contemplating something.

"No" Buret said "There is no advantage in waiting any longer, I will be receiving no other help, and for all I know you have friends that will come looking for you. It is time." He reached down and began unlatching each crystal one at a time and asked his people to distribute them around the room. They had no idea what they were doing, but they were helping Buret set up for the final spell. He was about to turn Nexus into a necropolis.

Buret turned to me and said "I was just going to suck your mind and soul away, but I will instead use you as my final sacrifice. Your energy will be greater than others here and will help fuel the final spell."

Without hesitation he moved to the center of the room. I had gotten most of my feeling back and began fiddling with the Fex cuffs. Fex technology was incredibly complex, which made it difficult override, but not difficult to break. I had learned ways to do it over time and was getting ready to do so, but I was not working fast enough.

I felt a cold sensation and I saw the shadows of the room creep toward me. I could feel fear, not from myself but from Buret's agents. Apparently, they had never been here during a ritual and this time was going to be the ritual of them all. The whole room went dark and then the crystals of the dome began to brightly glow purple and green. I could see all 27 Captiol Crystals being drawn on for this spell. The shadows continued to creep toward me and in the middle Buret held out his arms chanting the same phrase as Bo had been.

A choirs of voices came up from the bodies in the room and the chanting began to resonate. This seemed to freak the thugs out even further. Emin made a discreet exit from the Chamber. I was very close, I just needed the right moment.

That is when Buret suddenly triggered the ritual. It was sudden enough that I had not seen it coming and happened earlier than expected. This was it and I had not the time to get my cuffs off. There was something however that Buret did not know. You see, in this game there is always the thing you don't know. I was screwed by that a few minutes earlier and now it was Buret's turn. When I had opened the chest I knew I had discovered something that I had not known. Instead of panicking I changed the odds. I had used my illusion kit to create a fake chest with the fake crystals in it. The kit had "created" a fake chest with the crystals in it that could be opened, touched, and act as a physical object would. It was a weird combination of conjuring and illusion now that I think about it. Point was, the real chest was in my pocket of holding, and Buret was drawing off of nothing. If you put everything into a spell and did not have the energy you expected, you would hurt yourself. With Emin's addition, it was like pulling every muscle in your body at once.

Buret fell to the ground exhaling as he did out of pain. He balled up and the shadows retreated immediately. The room returned to its normal lighting and the thugs stood confused. One of them, a meat head of a Braxin asked "Is that what is supposed to happen?"

This was my moment. I made a final push to disarm the shackles. I couldn't act on Buret without doing so first since it likely would cripple me in pain if I did not remove them. Buret slowly recovered and took a deep breath. *Almost there...*

Buret went to stand up as he breathed in and as he stood looked... confused. He tried to exhale and acted as if he couldn't, as if his airways were blocked, but they were not. A moment earlier, Spark had entered the room and had in a sense attacked Buret. Buret had breathed Spark into his lungs to be exact. I heard Sparks voice, not in my head but in the room. "You bunch of chumps! Too Easy!" Spark didn't punch Buret or rip anyone to shreds, he just expanded… in Buret's lungs. Buret looked horrified and in great pain as his chest expanded, ribs cracking. It looked almost cartoon like, but by the end of it Buret was laying dead on the ground. His collapsed body looked like a Burrick had sat on his chest.

I got the cuffs off. I dropped them to the ground and looked around before grabbing at my blade. Something was wrong. Everyone in the room was not staring at me, nor even at Burets body, but at Bo's. Bo's dried up corpse began to twitch and move. It pushed its' arms out and lifted itself up, and spoke. "You mindless minions, I don't pay you to gawk, kill him!" And the corpse pointed at me. The Brax panicked and began firing… At Bo. Bo's chest and part of an arm vaporized, and the body fell limp on the ground.

The Brax then dropped his gun and held his hands to his head looking confused. *What the Hell is going on!?* I thought. Spark had an answer without me asking "For the love of all that is mortal Lagard, Buret was possessed! Kill them all!"

I could see a whirling wind pick up and it began passing around crushing and ripping apart the dried corpses. I took care of the living. I pulled out my blade and darted to the side of the Brax. What was now possessing the Brax tried grabbing at me, but it was obvious he didn't know his own reach. I came in under his arms and sliced under his armpit, opening an artery up. I then stabbed at his spine crippling his legs. I rolled out of the way and sought my next target. Raptor was raising her personal energy shield, but it was a mistake. She should have been shooting at me instead. I crossed the distance faster than she could react and my blade sung through her barrier. I went straight for her and I pierced her lower chest, right were a Hizarin's heart was.

There were only two remaining and one of them just ran out of the room. The other one, who had just been possessed as well, pulled out a grenade and lobbed it at me and Raptor. I had no shield so likely the grenade would kill me, so I used Raptor, who's shield was still active and intact as a body block. No need however, as a sudden gust of wind blew the grenade back, hitting the hired help in the chest. The grenade exploded, his shield flared with the excess energy burning his face and arms. I sprang forward into a full sprint, wind on my back, and lunged at him knocking him down. I stabbed at his neck and then at his chest. It was not as clean of a kill as the others were capable of, but I am a thief not an assassin.

I pulled myself off of the body and turned to the room. I could see a cloudy figure form in a humanoid shape. It was Spark. Before Spark could speak a horrifying scream echoed through the room. We both turned to see another figure forming, this time a specter of some kind. It looked like an Elf dressed in ancient philosopher's robes. The figure screamed and just vanished. Without anything to possess in this room and me soon taking the mana away from this place I could only assume it would wander the halls and dissolve. Spark did not seem fussed by anything that had occurred. Turning away from where the ghost had just been, he shrugged and spoke to me "Well I guess he is not going to try and possess you then, it looks like he just sort of fucked off. That was weird. Regardless, well done, let's get our loot out of here!" I smiled, I was much happier about stopping sealed kingdom 2 and you know, my own damned death along with it. But I responded with "Yeah, lets get our loot out of here before, but we have to make it past the hired help.

"Don't worry, Oochick is setting some sort of evacuation alarm on to all but this room."

"Oochick lives?"

"Yeah it was actually sort of funny. He was a such a large amount of data that he was just patiently sitting there in they system getting erased line by line. Like I said, I really don't think he is sentient."

"Well thanks for coming down here to save my ass."

"Your welcome boss! Well, I am going to head back to the security room and guide you out. I will put Oochick on a chip and bring him with us if that is alright."

"Yeah, it is." I smiled.

"Ok so I was thinking of calling the Nexus authorities from the security station, what do you think?"

I thought about it for a moment. "You know, we have acquired some wealth here, but we only have grabbed half the riches."

"Wait, what!?" Spark seemed to panic at this. "Is there a secret room or something, I mean I am pretty sure I got everything of value that was out and about."

"No" I smiled again. "That is not the wealth I mean. There are a lot of hired hands here that are very expensive. Most of their bounties are too. Send, instead, this location onto Grumgal, I owe her for not ratting me out to SA authorities last year. Seal the elevator and prepare to disable it once we reach the top."

"Great! The Huntsman Guild will have to put some work in chasing this scum through the surrounding areas, but they will love it."

I nodded and we got to work. I avoided the crowd at the elevator by crawling in through the top and cutting my way into it. All three of us rode to the top and then disabled the elevator. I had no doubt the Huntsman guild would be here soon with some heavy hitters of their own ready to nab bad guys and save slaves. This was a gift that would keep Grumgal satisfied and a debt to her paid in full.

The trip back to our headquarters was not long. One of our guild members was able to pick us up and take us back. After the shock of survival wore off, I stopped to appreciate how much we had looted the place for. When Spark had reentered my suit, he actually felt heavy. I mean come on, he was likely using a dimensional pocket to store the stuff, how much was he carrying? After we got back to headquarters, I gave the Capitol Crystals to the bookkeeper who in turn placed them in the vault. As was tradition, Spark stored his goods in my personal vault, as everyone thought he was a non-sentient AI. I have pretty big vault, but I am pretty sure ninty-percent of it is cheap junk Spark has picked up over the years. He hates selling his goods, and just collects it indefinitely. I on the other hand enjoy a select few highly valuable items, though most of those have been exchanged in to fuel the guild. I have already traded several of the crystals, and through them I have made the guild absurdly powerful. That one mission has defined our standing since, which can happen sometimes.

Well, there you have it. That is the full of the tale and I hope you learned something from it. Don't underestimate the cluster, always be prepared to react to the unexpected, and be patient. Whoever you are, whatever your goals are, I wish you luck. If we do cross paths you may not know it.

-Lagard the Unseen